One of India's ...
**Rabindranath Tag**...
of the world when his *Gitanjali* was awarded the Nobel Prize for literature in 1913. A poet's poet, he is a maker of not only modern Indian literature but also the modern Indian mind. Myriad-minded, he was a poet, short story writer, novelist, dramatist, essayist, painter and composer of songs. Gandhi called him the 'Great Sentinel'. His world-wide acclaim as a social, political, religious and aesthetic thinker, innovator in education and a champion of the 'One World' idea makes him a living presence.

This book was posthumously published in 1944. **'The Parrot's Training'** (*Tota-Kahini*) is one of Tagore's finest satires criticising the contemporary education system. 'Great News' (*Bado Khabar*) is a portion of the dialogue taken from *Galpa-Shalpa*, a unique collection of tales and fancies. 'The Old Man's Ghost' *(Kartar Bhut)* deals with an unreasonable dread of change. The first story is translated by Tagore himself, the second by Surendranath Tagore and the last two by Amiya Chakravarty.

RABINDRA RACHANAVALI

# The Parrot's Training & Other Stories

Rabindranath Tagore

Rupa & Co

*Sales Centres:*
Allahabad Bangalore Chandigarh Chennai
Dehradun Hyderabad Jaipur Kathmandu
Kolkata Ludhiana Mumbai Pune



Design & Typeset by
Arrt Creations
45 Nehru Apts, Kalkaji
New Delhi 110 019

Printed in India by
Gopsons Papers Ltd.,
A-14 Sector 60
Noida 201 301

*page ii:*
Rabindranath Tagore in the role of Valmiki in the play *Valmiki Prativa*
*page vi:*
Signed 'Sri Rabindra' in Bengali. No date. Ink on paper. 25 x 20.4 cm

# Contents

# The Parrot's Training

Once upon a time there was a bird. It was ignorant. It sang all right, but never recited scriptures. It hopped pretty frequently, but lacked manners.

Said the Raja to himself: "Ignorance is costly in the long run. For fools consume as much food as their betters, and yet give nothing in return."

He called his nephews to his presence and told them that the bird must have a sound schooling.

The pundits were summoned, and at once went to the root of the matter. They decided that the ignorance of birds was due to their natural habit

of living in poor nests. Therefore, according to the pundits, the first thing necessary for this bird's education was a suitable cage.

The pundits had their rewards and went home happy.

A golden cage was built with gorgeous decorations. Crowds came to see it from all parts of the world.

"Culture, captured and caged!" exclaimed some, in a rapture of ecstasy, and burst into tears.

Others remarked: "Even if culture be missed, the cage will remain, to the end, a substantial fact. How fortunate for the bird!"

The goldsmith filled his bag with money and lost no time in sailing homewards.

The pundit sat down to educate the bird. With proper deliberation he took his pinch of snuff, as he said: "Textbooks can never be too many for our purpose!"

The nephews brought together an enormous crowd of scribes. They copied from books, and copied from copies, till the manuscripts were piled up to an unreachable height.

Men murmured in amazement: "Oh, the tower of culture, egregiously high! The end of it lost in the clouds!"

The scribes, with light hearts, hurried home, their pockets heavily laden.

The nephews were furiously busy keeping the cage in proper trim.

As their constant scrubbing and polishing went on, the people said with satisfaction: "This is progress indeed!"

Men were employed in large numbers, and supervisors were still more numerous. These, with their cousins of all different degrees of distance, built a palace for themselves and lived there happily ever after.

Whatever may be its other deficiencies, the world is never in want of fault-finders; and they went about saying that every creature remotely connected with the cage flourished beyond words, excepting only the bird.

When this remark reached the Raja's ears, he summoned his nephews before him and said: "My dear nephews, what is this that we hear?"

The nephews said in answer: "Sire, let the testimony of the goldsmiths and the pundits, the scribes and the supervisors, be taken, if the truth is to be known. Food is scarce with the fault-finders, and that is why their tongues have gained in sharpness."

The explanation was so luminously satisfactory that the Raja decorated each one of his nephews with his own rare jewels.

The Raja at length, being desirous of seeing with his own eyes how his Education Department busied itself with the little bird, made his appearance one day at the great Hall of Learning.

From the gate rose the sounds of conch-shells and gongs, horns, bugles and trumpets, cymbals, drums and kettledrums, tomtoms, tambourines, flutes, fifes, barrel-organs and bagpipes. The pundits began chanting *mantras* with their topmost voices, while the goldsmiths, scribes, supervisors, and their numberless cousins of all different degrees of distance, loudly raised a round of cheers.

The nephews smiled and said: "Sire, what do you think of it all?"

The Raja said : "It does seem so fearfully like a sound principle of Education!"

Mightily pleased, the Raja was about to remount his elephant, when the fault-finder, from behind some bush, cried out: "Maharaja, have you seen the bird?"

"Indeed, I have not!" exclaimed the Raja, "I completely forgot about the bird."

Turning back, he asked the pundits about the method they followed in instructing the bird.

It was shown to him. He was immensely impressed. The method was so stupendous that the bird looked ridiculously unimportant in comparison. The Raja was satisfied that there was no flaw in the arrangements. As for any complaint from the bird itself, that simply could not be expected. Its throat was so completely choked with the leaves from the books that it could neither whistle nor whisper. It sent a thrill through one's body to watch the process.

This time, while remounting his elephant, the Raja ordered his State Ear-puller to give a thorough good pull at both the ears of the fault-finder.

The bird thus crawled on, duly and properly, to the safest verge of inanity. In fact, its progress

was satisfactory in the extreme. Nevertheless, nature occasionally triumphed over training, and when the morning light peeped into the bird's cage it sometimes fluttered its wings in a reprehensible manner. And, though it is hard to believe, it pitifully pecked at its bars with its feeble beak.

"What impertinence!" growled the kotwal.

The blacksmith, with his forge and hammer took his place in the Raja's Department of Education. Oh, what resounding blows! The iron chain was soon completed, and the bird's wings were clipped.

The Raja's brothers-in-law looked black, and shook their heads, saying: "These birds not only lack good sense, but also gratitude!"

With text-book in one hand and baton in the other, the pundits gave the poor bird what may fitly be called lessons!

The kotwal was honoured with a title for his watchfulness, and the blacksmith for his skill in forging chains.

The bird died.

Nobody had the least notion how long ago this had happened. The fault-finder was the first man to spread the rumour.

The Raja called his nephews and asked them: "My dear nephews, what is this that we hear?"

The nephews said: "Sire, the bird's education has been completed."

"Does it hop?" the Raja enquired.

"Never!" said the nephews.

"Does it fly?"

"No."

"Bring me the bird," said the Raja.

The bird was brought to him, guarded by the kotwal and the sepoys and the sowars. The Raja poked its body with his finger. Only its inner stuffing of book-leaves rustled.

Outside the window, the murmur of the spring breeze amongst the newly budded *asoka* leaves made the April, morning wistful.

# The Trial of the Horse

Brahma, the creator, was very near the end of his task of creation when a new idea struck him.

He sent for the Store-keeper and said: "O keeper of the stores, bring to my factory a quantity of each of the five elements. For I am ready to create another creature."

"Lord of the universe," the Storekeeper replied, "when in the first flush of creative extravagance you began to turn out such exaggerations as elephants and whales and pythons and tigers, you took no count of the stock. Now, all the elements that have density and force are nearly used up.

The supply of earth and water and fire has become inconveniently scanty, while of air and ether there is as much as is good for us and a good deal more."

The four-headed deity looked perplexed and pulled at his four pairs of moustaches. At last he said: "The limitedness of material gives all the more scope to originality. Send me whatever you have left."

This time BRAHMA was excessively sparing with the earth, water and fire. The new creature was not given either horns or claws, and his teeth were only meant for chewing, not for biting. The prudent care with which fire was used in his formation made him necessary in war without making him warlike.

This animal was the Horse.

The reckless expenditure of air and ether, which went into his composition, was amazing. And, in consequence, he perpetually struggled to outreach the wind, to outrun space itself. The other animals run only when they have a reason, but the horse would run for nothing whatever, as if to run out of his own skin. He had no desire to chase, or to kill, but only to fly on and on till he dwindled into a dot, melted into a swoon, blurred into a shadow, and vanished into vacancy.

The CREATOR was glad. He had given for his other creatures habitations,—to some the forests, to others the caves. But in his enjoyment of the disinterested spirit of speed in the Horse, he gave him an open meadow under the very eye of heaven.

By the side of this meadow lived Man.

Man has his delight in pillaging and piling things up. And he is never happy till these grow into a burden. So, when he saw this new creature pursuing the wind and kicking at the sky, he said to himself: "If only I can bind and secure this Horse, I can use his broad back for carrying my loads."

So one day he caught the Horse.

Then man put a saddle on the Horse's back and a spiky bit in his mouth. He regularly had hard rubbing and scrubbing to keep him fit, and there were the whip and spurs to remind him that it was wrong to have his own will.

Man also put high walls round the Horse, lest if left at large in the open the creature might escape him.

So it came to pass, that while the Tiger who had his forest remained in the the forest, the Lion who had his cave remained in the cave, the Horse who once had his open meadow came to spend his days in a stable. Air and ether had roused in the horse longings for deliverance, but they swiftly delivered him into bondage.

When he felt that bondage did not suit him, the Horse kicked at the stable walls.

But this hurt his hoofs much more than it hurt the wall. Still some of the plaster came off and the wall lost its beauty.

Man felt aggrieved.

"What ingratitude!" he cried. "Do I not give him food and drink ? Do I not keep highly-paid men-servants to watch over him day and night? Indeed he is hard to please."

In their desperate attempts to please the Horse, the men-servants fell upon him and so vigorously applied all their winning methods that he lost his power to kick and a great deal more besides.

Then Man called his friends and neighbours together, and said to them exultingly: "Friends, did you ever see so devoted a steed as mine ?"

"Never!" they replied. "He seems as still as ditch water and as mild as the religion you profess."

The Horse, as is well known, had no horns, no claws, nor adequate teeth, at his birth. And, when on the top of this, all kicking at the walls and even into emptiness had been stopped, the only way to give vent to his feelings was to neigh.

But that disturbed Man's sleep.

Moreover, this neighing was not likely to impress the neighbours as a pæan of devotion and thankfulness. So Man invented devices to shut the Horse's mouth.

But the voice cannot be altogether suppressed so long as the mistake is made of leaving any breath in the body. Therefore a spasmodic sound of moaning came from his throat now and then.

One day this noise reached BRAHMA'S ears.

The CREATOR woke up from his meditation. It gave him a start when he glanced at the meadow and saw no sign of the Horse.

"This is all your doing," cried BRAHMA, in anger to Yama, the god of death : "You have taken away the Horse!"

"Lord of all creatures!" Death replied : "All your worst suspicions you keep only for me. But most of the calamities in your beautiful world will be explained if you turn your eyes in the direction of Man."

BRAHMA looked below. He saw a small enclosure, walled in, from which the dolorous moaning of his Horse came fitfully.

BRAHMA frowned in anger.

"Unless you set free my Horse," said he: "I shall take care that he grows teeth and claws like the Tiger."

"That would be ungodly," cried man: "to encourage ferocity. All the same, if I may speak plain truth about a creature of your own make, this Horse is not fit to be set free. It was for his eternal good that I built him this stable—this marvel of architecture."

BRAHMA remained obdurate.

"I bow to your wisdom," said Man: "but if, after seven days, you still think that your meadow is better for him than my stable, I will humbly own defeat."

After this Man set to work.

He made the Horse go free, but hobbled his front legs. The result was so vastly diverting that it was enough to make even a frog burst his sides with laughter.

BRAHMA, from the height of his heaven, could see the comic gait of his Horse, but not the tragic rope which hobbled him. He was mortified to find his own creature openly exposing its divine maker to ridicule.

"It was an absurd blunder of mine", he cried, "closely touching the sublime."

"Grandsire," said Man with a pathetic show of sympathy, "what can I do for this unfortunate creature? If there is a meadow in your heaven, I am willing to take trouble to transport him thither."

"Take him back to your stable!" cried BRAHMA in dismay.

"Merciful God!" cried Man, "what a great burden it will be for mankind!"

"It is the burden of humanity," muttered BRAHMA.

# Old Man's Ghost

At the time of the Old Man Leader's death, the entire population wailed, "What will be our lot when you go?"

Hearing this, the Old Man himself felt sad. "Who indeed," thought he, "will keep these people quiescent when I have gone?"

Death cannot be evaded, however. Yet the gods took pity and said: "Why worry? Let this fellow go on sitting on their shoulders even as a ghost. Man dies but a ghost does not."

The people of the country were greatly relieved.

For, worries come if only you believe in a future. Believing in ghosts you are freed from burden, all the worries enter the ghost's head. Yet the ghost has no head, so it does not suffer from headaches either, not for anybody's sake.

Those, who out of sheer wrong habit still attempt to think for themselves, get their ears boxed by the ghost. From this ghostly boxing you can neither free yourself nor can you escape it; against it is neither appeal nor any judgment at all.

The entire population, ghost-ridden, now walks with eyes shut. "The most ancient form of movement this, with eyes shut," the philosophers assure them, "moving like blind fate, we call it. Thus moved the first eyeless amoeba. In the grass, in the trees, this habit of movement is still customary."

Hearing which, the ghost-ridden land feels its own primitive aristocracy. And it is greatly delighted.

The Ghost's *nayeb* is the inspector of the prison. The walls of the prison-house are not visible to the eye. And so it is impossible to imagine how to pierce those walls and get free.

In the prison-house one has to slave at turning the oil-press night and day but not even an ounce of oil is produced which is marketable; only the energy of men goes out in extracting the oil. When their energy goes out, men become exceedingly peaceful. And thus in that ghost's realm whatever else there might not be—food, or clothing or health—tranquillity remains.

How great is the tranquillity is proved by one example: in other lands excessive ghostly tyranny makes men restless and seek for a medicine-man. Here such a thought cannot arise. For the medicine-man himself has already been possessed by the ghost.

Thus the days would have passed; nobody would have questioned the ghostly administration. Forever they could have taken pride that their future, like a pet lamb, was tied to the ghost's peg such a creature neither bleated nor baad, it sprawled dumb on the dust, useless as dust.

Only, for a slight reason, some little trouble arose. It was that the other countries of the world were not ghost-ridden. Their oil-presses turned so that the extracted oil might be used for keeping the wheels of men's chariots moving forward, not for crushing the heart and pouring heart's blood into the paws of the ghost. So, men there have not yet been completely pacified. They were terribly wakeful.

All over the ghostly empire: *the baby sleeps; quiet is the neighbourhood.*

That is comforting for the baby, and for the baby's guardian too; as to the neighbourhood, we have already seen how it is.

But there is the other line, "*the invaders enter the land.*"

Thus the rhythm is completed—otherwise for lack of one foot, this history would have been crippled.

The pedants and pundits are asked : "Why is it thus ?"

They toss their heads together and say: "Not the ghost's fault this, nor of the ghost-ridden land : the fault lies with the invader. Why does the invader come ?"

"How right!" they all admit. And everyone feels exceedingly comforted.

Whosever the fault might be, near the back-door of the house loiter the ghost's emissaries, and in the open street outside everywhere roam the non-ghost's emissaries; the householder can hardly stay in his house, to stir out of doors is also impossible. From one side they shout "pay the taxes!" and from the other also they shout "pay the taxes!"

Now the problem is, *"how to pay the taxes?"*

Up to now, from north, south, east and west, bulbulis of all species have come in large flocks, and gorged themselves with the corn, nobody was mindful. With all those who are mindful, these people avoid contact, lest they have to do *prayashchitta* for contamination. But those other folk who are mindful have a way of coming suddenly very near to them indeed and they do not observe any penance either.

The pedants and pundits open the text and say: "Pure are the unmindful, and impure the mindful ones; so be indifferent to these latter. Remember the sacred words, 'awake are those who sleepeth.'"

And hearing this the people are hugely delighted.

But, in spite of this, the query cannot be stopped, *"how to pay the taxes?"*

From the burning-ground, from the burial-ground the wild winds bring the loud answer: "Pay the taxes with the price of your modesty, with your honour, with your conscience, with your heart's blood."

The trouble with questions is: when they come they do not come singly. So, another question has arisen : "Will the ghostly reign itself remain for ever?"

Hearing this, all the lullaby-singing aunts and uncles put their hands on their ears in horror and exclaim: "Perdition! Never in our fathers' life have we heard of such a thing! What will then have happened to our sleep, the most ancient sleep, the sleep which is earlier than all awakening?"

"That I see", the questioner persists: "but these most modern flocks of bulbulis and these very much present invaders— what about *them*?"

"To the bulbulis we shall repeat the name of Krishna," assert the aunts and uncles, "and so shall we do to the invaders."

The ignorant youths get impertinent and bluster out: "Drive the ghost out we shall— whatever the means."

The ghost's *nayeb* rolls his eyes in anger and shouts, "Shut up! The oil-press hasn't stopped grinding. No, not yet."

Hearing which the baby of the land falls silent, and then turns to sleep.

The great fact is, the Old Man is neither alive nor dead, but is a ghost. He neither stirs the country up nor ever relaxes his grip.

Inside the country, one or two men— those who never utter a word in daytime for fear of the *nayeb*— join their palms together and implore: "Old Man Leader, is it not yet time for you to leave us ?"

"You fool," answers the Old Man, "I neither hold, nor let go; if you leave, then I have also left."

"But we are afraid, Old Man Leader!"

"That is where the ghost enters."— comes the answer.

# Great News

Said Kusmi: "You would give me all the big news—so you promised, didn't you, Dadamashay? How else could I get educated ?"

Answered Dadamashay: "But such a sack of big news there would be to carry— with so much of rubbish in it."

"Why not leave those out."

"Little else would remain, then. And that remainder you will think as small news. But that would be the real news."

"Give it to me— the real news."

"So I will."

"Well, Dadamashay, let me see what skill you have. Tell me the great news of these days, making it ever so small."

"Listen".

Work was proceeding in peace.

In a mahajani boat there started a row between the sail and the oars.

The oars came clattering to the court of the Boatman, and said: "This cannot be endured any longer. That braggart sail of yours, swelling himself, calls us *chhoto lok.* Because we, tied night and day to the lower planks, must toil, pushing the waters as we proceed, while he moves by whim, not caring for the push of any one's hand. And so he is a *bara lok.* You must decide who is more worthy. If we are *chhoto lok*, the inferior ones, we shall resign in a body. Let us see how you make your boat move."

The Boatman, seeing danger ahead, called the oars aside and whispered secretly: "Do not give ear to his words, brothers. He speaks an empty language, that sail. If you strong fellows did not work away, staking life and death, the boat would lie inert altogether. And that sail—he sits there in hallow luxury, perched on the top. At the slightest touch of stormy wind he flops, folds himself up, and lies low on the boat's thatch. Then all his vain flutterings are silenced, not a word from him at all. But in weal and woe, in danger and in crisis, on the way to the market and the ghat, you are my constant support. It is a pity that you have to carry that useless burden of luxury, to and fro. Who says you are *chhoto lok.*"

But the Boatman was afraid, lest these words be overheard by the sail. So he came to him and whispered into his ear : "Mr. Sail, none ever can be compared with you. Who says that you drive the boat, that is the work of labourers. You move at your own pleasure, and your pals and comrades follow you at your slightest gesture and bidding. And whenever you feel out of breath, you would flop down easefully, and rest. Do not lend your ear, friend, to the parleying of those low-bred oars; so firmly have I tied them up, that splutter as they might, they cannot but work as slaves."

Hearing this, the sail stretched himself, and yawned mightily.

But the signs were not good. Those oars are hard-boned fellows, now they lie aslant but who knows when they will stand up straight, slap at the sail and shatter his pride into shreds. Then the world would know that it is the oars who make the boat move, come storm come tornado, whether it be upstream or at ebb-tide.

Queried Kusmi: "Your big news, is it so small as this? You are joking."

Said Dadamashay: "Joking it seems to be. Very soon this news will become big indeed."

"And then?"

"Then your Dadamashay will practise keeping time with the strokes of those oars."

"And I ?"

"Where the oars creak too much, you will pour a drop of oil."

Dadamashay continued : "True news appears small, like the seeds. And then comes the tree

with its branches and foliage. Do you understand now?"

"So I do," said Kusmi. Her face showed that she had not understood. But Kusmi had one virtue, she would not easily admit it to her Dadamashay that she would not understand. That she is less clever than *Iru Mashi* is better kept concealed.

# Glossary

*Bulbuli*—A species of Indian nightingale; these birds often do great harm to the crops.

The social significance of this folksong is brought out in a popular Bengali nursery rhyme:

"The baby sleeps, the neighbourhood is quiet;
The invaders enter the land;
The *bulbulis* have eaten the corn,
How to pay the taxes?"

*Chhotolok*—Literally iterally, small people; a common term used abusingly with regard to the working classes by the so-called "big people", or "*bara-lok*".

*Dadamashay*—Grandfather.

*Iru Mashi*—Aunt Iru (Mashi—mother's sister).

*Kotwal*—Chief of the Police.

*Mahajani boat*—Boat for carrying merchandise.

*Mantras*—sacred texts from ancient Hindu scriptures, which are often to be found in abbreviated verse-form.

*Nayeb*—Manager.

*Prayashchitta*—Penance and purification.

*Pundit*—Pedant.

# notes